This Mammoth
belongs to

_____

_____

_____

First published in Great Britain 1969
by William Heinemann Limited
This edition 1999 by Mammoth
an imprint of Egmont Children's Books Limited
239 Kensington High Street, London, W8 6SL

10 9 8 7 6 5 4 3 2 1

Text copyright © Margaret Mahy 1969, 1991
Illustrations copyright © Helen Oxenbury 1969, 1991

ISBN 0 7497 3742 5

A CIP catalogue record for this title is available from the British Library

Printed in the U.A.E.

The Dragon *of an* Ordinary Family

story by Margaret Mahy

pictures by Helen Oxenbury

There was this family called Belsaki . . . Mr Belsaki, Mrs Belsaki, and their little boy, Orlando Belsaki. They were quite ordinary people, their house was a quite ordinary house in a quite ordinary street – and no doubt they would have lived quite ordinary lives forever, if one morning Mrs Belsaki hadn't called Mr Belsaki a FUDDY-DUDDY.

It was like this:

The day began with breakfast, as usual, with Mr Belsaki rushing through his hot oatmeal, a little late for work, as usual. Just as he was rushing out of the door, hat and briefcase in hand, Mrs Belsaki called after him, "On your way home, dear, stop in at the pet shop and buy Orlando a pet."

"A pet!" exclaimed Mr Belsaki. "What does he want a pet for? We haven't the room, anyway."

"Nonsense!" snapped Mrs Belsaki. "Of *course* we can have a pet. And we have room for an ELEPHANT, if Orlando wanted one."

"An ELEPHANT!" Mr Belsaki turned slightly pale and his mouth hung open in a foolish fashion.

"All right, all right," Mrs Belsaki said impatiently, "he doesn't *want* an elephant, as it happens. He just wants a puppy – or perhaps a little kitten . . . Don't be a FUDDY-DUDDY, Mr Belsaki!"

Mr Belsaki stamped out crossly, pulling his hat down over his ears, muttering "Fuddy-duddy, fuddy-duddy, indeed!"

On his way home from work, Mr Belsaki went into the pet shop and looked around. He saw white mice and hamsters, puppies and kittens, all shapes and kinds of birds, some sad-eyed goldfish, and a parrot called Joe, with a sign over him saying NOT FOR SALE.

Mr Belsaki glowered at them all and glared around the shop.

Then his eye caught a sign which said UNUSUAL PET, VERY CHEAP. In smaller lettering underneath, it said DRAGON, HOUSE-TRAINED, 50p.

"That is very reasonable," said Mr Belsaki to the pet shop man. "I suppose it isn't a very good breed of dragon."

The pet shop man sighed. "No, it's a good breed – the *only* breed," he explained. "But it's a very small one . . . And, too, there isn't much demand, you know."

Mr Belsaki hesitated, and the dragon blinked his violet-blue eyes at him and flicked his tongue out.

"I'll take it!" said Mr Belsaki loudly.

And that was how it happened that he came home with a tiny dragon in a shoe box.

"What on earth is in *there*?" Mrs Belsaki asked, surprised at the noisy snuffles coming from the shoe box.

"A dragon," replied Mr Belsaki triumphantly.

"A *dragon*!" Mrs Belsaki screamed.

"A DRAGON!" cried Orlando in delight.

"It was cheap," Mr Belsaki answered, clutching the shoe box to him as if he were afraid that Mrs Belsaki might snatch it away. "You said I was a FUDDY-DUDDY," he added firmly, "and I am no such thing!"

"You could have chosen something *pretty*," Mrs Belsaki complained. "A ginger kitten perhaps, or a budgie-bird that talks . . . Where will we *keep* a dragon?"

"We have room enough here to keep an ELEPHANT," Mr Belsaki reminded her.

So they kept the dragon, and it grew and grew.

It was a wonderful pet for Orlando. He kept it in the shoe box for a while, then in a bird cage, then in a dog kennel. He painted a washtub for its food, with the word DRAGON on it in red.

The dragon grew and grew. Mrs Belsaki became quite proud of it. "It certainly gives a different look to the place," she said at least once a day. "It makes us a bit out of the ordinary."

Her friends said, "What on earth did he get *that* for?" But Mrs Belsaki always replied, "Mr Belsaki's a man with *ideas*, that's why!" And she always added, "He's not a FUDDY-DUDDY – not like some."

The dragon grew and grew.
Finally it filled the whole yard.
It got so it could breathe out smoke
and fire.

It even got big enough for Orlando to ride.

Then it even got as big as an elephant. None of Mrs Belsaki's friends came to visit any more. They were rather afraid.

The dragon grew . . .

It grew *bigger* than an elephant!

It grew TOO big!

One day the Mayor came to look at the Belsaki's dragon. He studied it and studied it.

"It is *much* too big to keep in a built-up area," he said crossly. "Mr Belsaki, you are just an ordinary family, and you should stick to ordinary pets. Mr Belsaki, you must sell it . . . to a zoo. Or to a circus . . . Or to a handbag factory. Some people would pay a lot for dragon-skin."

Mr and Mrs Belsaki looked very worried and sad. They loved their dragon, but, beyond all doubt, it *was* growing too big. Besides, it cost so much to feed.

"We can't even afford to buy a Christmas tree, or go on holiday this year," Mr Belsaki said gloomily.

"Well, *I* would rather have our dragon!" Orlando cried.

"Well, you can't," the Mayor answered snappishly. "It is just too much! . . . You have exactly one week to get rid of it."

And he marched away.

"As if we would sell our dragon!" Mrs Belsaki said indignantly. "And we certainly don't want him made into a handbag! . . . Oh, if only we knew of a dragon-loving farmer. We could give him away to a really good farmer."

Then the dragon turned around and faced them. For the first time, he spoke. "As a matter of fact, it *is* getting a little cramped here for me, and I feel that, though I am fond of you all, I should shift to another place . . . How would you like to come with *me* for the Christmas holidays?"

"Where were you thinking of going?" Mr Belsaki asked cautiously.

"To the Isles of Magic," the dragon answered. "*All* dragons know the way there."

Mrs Belsaki thought a moment. "Well, it *could* be all right. I'll go and pack."

So the Mayor, and Mrs Belsaki's friends, and their ordinary neighbours were amazed to see Mr and Mrs Belsaki and Orlando fly away on the dragon's back, that very day – off for their holidays – with their suitcases and shopping bags and baskets and paper boxes tied to the dragon's tail.

Higher and higher the dragon flew – way up into the clouds – and then, after a long time, he dropped down, down, down – and there, below them, lay the bluest-blue sea, with the Isles of Magic spread across it, all gold and green as if summer leaves had been blown there by a dreaming wind.

Oh, the Isles of Magic! What would the Belsakis do on the Isles of Magic?

For the Isles of Magic, the dragon explained to them as they flew along, are the homes of all the wonderful, strange, fairy-tale people. What would an ordinary family with an ordinary home, with dustbins, a teapot, and a neat, mowed lawn – what would *they* do on the Isles of Magic?

This is what the Belsakis did:

They walked in the forests, the green and gold, the dark and old forests. They saw the starry towers of castles rising above the trees, and princesses sitting in the windows combing their hair, waiting for princes to come and rescue them. They met all manner of youngest sons – the youngest sons of kings, of millers, of cobblers and beggars – all seeking fortunes.

Some days they went sailing in a great galleon over shining seas, diving for pearls through deep, green water. They hunted and sailed with pirates, and buried treasure in golden sand on islands where parrots screamed and monkeys mocked in the palm trees. And all the while, the Belsakis could hear mermaids singing among the great, black rocks under the lacy veil of the spray.

On other days they searched for lost cities in deep, twining jungles – and found them, too! – cities of ivory, cities of gold, forgotten and terribly old . . . Or they watched witches twitch their broomsticks over the sky.

On the far horizon, like mountains, giants moved on their mysterious business. From the windows of the castle they lived in, the Belsaki family watched them curiously and nervously – and kept their distance.

When Christmas came they sang their carols around a tree covered in small candles accommodatingly formed by hundreds of glow-worms – so high that a real star shivered, fragile and far, on its top.

Mr Belsaki's best present was a special pipe that played strange, wild music. Mrs Belsaki got a sewing basket set with emeralds, and with an ivory thimble and little silver scissors shaped like a stork. Orlando got a chess set where little knights and queens and pawns came alive and chased one another all over the board.

At last the time came for them to go back home. The dragon stayed, for the Isles of Magic are the proper place for dragons.

Then the Belsaki family sailed off home on a flying carpet, and, as a farewell present, the dragon gave Orlando a tiny black kitten with an over-sized purr.

"Now," said Mrs Belsaki, her unpacking nearly done, as she looked lovingly around her kitchen, "we can settle down to be nice, ordinary people again. I'm very glad Mr Belsaki is *not* a FUDDY-DUDDY, and I was very fond of that dragon – but I must say it will be pleasant to relax with our neighbours again."

"Next Christmas," asked Orlando hopefully, "can we visit the Isles of Magic and see our dragon again?"

"Who knows," said Mrs Belsaki, a little wistfully, "we may never *see* him again . . ." Then she said, a little sadly, "I suppose we'll just have to settle down and *be* just an ordinary family. Perhaps no other magic will ever happen to us again."

Just then the little black kitten woke and sat up tall in Orlando's lap. "I wouldn't be too sure of that," he murmured, and went back to sleep.